P9-DUD-524

AND THE PEOPLE STAYED HOME

By **Kitty O'Meara**

Illustrated by
Stefano Di Cristofaro and **Paul Pereda**

 tra.publishing

And the people stayed home.

NO LONGER PROPERTY OF
SEATTLE PUBLIC LIBRARY

For Phillip, who makes staying home an endless,
surprising adventure, our few rooms a universe, and our life
together magical and holy. Thank you for keeping me joyful and
hopeful during the time of pandemic, and looking forward
to the days of bright sunlight to come.

—Kitty O'Meara

And they listened,

and read books,

and rested,

and exercised,

and made art,

and played games,

and learned new ways of being,

and were still.

And they listened more deeply.

Some meditated,

some prayed,

some danced.

Some met their shadows.

And the people began to think differently.

And the people healed.

And, in the absence of people living in ignorant, dangerous, and heartless ways, the earth began to heal.

And when the danger passed,

and the people joined together again,

they grieved their losses,

and made new choices,

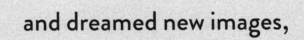
and dreamed new images,

and created new ways to live

and heal the earth fully,

as they had been healed.

Talking with Author Kitty O'Meara

And the People Stayed Home was written in the early days of the global coronavirus pandemic. For Kitty O'Meara, who lives in Wisconsin with her husband, Phillip, and their five dogs and three cats, life was quieter than usual. That slowing down gave Kitty time to think deeply about people and the planet.

One day, Kitty wrote a poem about what might happen during the pandemic and after it. She posted the poem on Facebook, and people all over the world loved it! Kitty's words teach us the importance of spending time with ourselves and the people close to us, listening deeply, and doing what we love. She believes that when we are kind to ourselves and others, and when we use the special gifts we each have, we can make the world a better place.

What led you to write this poem?

I was anxious because so many things about the virus weren't understood yet. I was worried about my family and my friends who work in hospitals. I was thinking about the quarantine and how it might affect us. And I was thinking about the earth. I care deeply about the earth. We depend on her for our food, and homes, and for beauty, too. We need to take care of the planet. We have been ignoring her, and she is not doing well without our love.

We are talking to each other while COVID-19 is causing us to stay at home. But there are some good things about this time, too, as your poem describes. What are some of them?

I think it is a time to go deep inside of ourselves and listen to what we are thinking and feeling. If we are scared, sad, happy, or angry, we can dance about it, compose a song, paint a picture, talk with our family, write a play. There are many things we can do. We have the gift of time to explore our feelings, to figure out what our talents are, learn more about what we love, and offer our talents to each other and the earth. The virus brings sickness, but we can choose to be more alive than ever. We can rest. We can sit and listen to the birds, and make art, learn something new, share family stories, or plant a flower seed and watch it grow, day by day.

After you wrote the poem, it spread quickly on the Internet. You heard from people around the world who love it. People from India, Italy, Spain, South America, Africa, and so many other places. Can you talk about that?

A great source of joy has been the people from all over the world who have interpreted the poem using their gifts—music, art, dance, and more. There has been a ballet with people narrating in eight languages. A children's choir in Italy sang it. Two people filmed themselves singing it on a rooftop in Spain. A famous opera star sang an original work based on it! And it has been translated into so many languages—more than twenty. I have new friends all over the world thanks to this poem. I want to hug them all.

What are your days like during quarantine?

Our four-leggeds get us up. We walk the dogs, then we feed them and have a Morning Party. Phillip, my husband, goes into his shop where he builds furniture. And I write. We also spend a lot of time in our gardens.

Your four-leggeds are your five rescue dogs and three cats. What are their names?

The dogs are Gracie, Micky, Marlarky, Dooley, and Teagan. (Gracie and Teagan are girls.) The cats are Fiona, Murphy (we also call him Bunny Bundles), and Fergus, who is a little blond stray that followed me home one chilly November day.

When did you start writing?

I have written since I was six years old—stories, poems, and book manuscripts. And I was always reading. My mother and father both read to us. As soon as I could read, trips to the library were the most magical adventures in the universe.

What were you like as a kid?

I loved school. I did a lot of inventing. I was athletic, and I was confident. I've always loved to laugh. I liked to write plays and then direct them. I was always writing. And every summer I had a little garden. I loved my friends, and being kind has always been important to me. I've never been a bully, and I do not like it when other people behave like bullies.

What are you like now?

I love learning. I'm a good friend. I love to cook and bake and make candy. I make caramels and toffee and fudge. I love the earth. I love life. Being an artist, I am never satisfied with what is given. I want to change and recreate. I write, take photographs, and garden. I adore being with my husband and our four-leggeds.

What would you say to a kid who wants to be a writer or an artist?

Do it! Read a lot, and keep a journal. Start thinking about things from different points of view. Bring in as many of the arts as you can. How would I dance that? How would I draw it? And don't judge! Just create. Do what you love and learn from other artists. We are students all our lives.

Is there anything else you would like to say to your readers?

I want to remind people that they are already artists. Art is not for only a few people. Any job, anything you do can be art. It is the attention and grace you offer it. It's about talent, beauty, generosity of spirit, innovation, and your humanity. Find your art and offer it to the world. And be kind; always try to be kind, and feed your joy.

Kitty O'Meara

lives in Full Moon Cottage, near Madison, Wisconsin, on a river and a bike trail, with her husband, Phillip Hagedorn, their five dogs, three cats, gardens, and books. A former teacher and chaplain and a spiritual director, O'Meara has been a lifelong writer and artist. *And the People Stayed Home* is her first print book.

Stefano Di Cristofaro

is an illustrator and designer whose works have been widely exhibited. Raised in Venezuela and Italy, he currently lives and works in Mexico City. He has previously illustrated the children's books *Conejo y Conejo*, *Guachipira va de viaje*, and *La Sayona y otros cuentos de espantos*. His family says that when he was little, he only stayed still if he was given a pencil and a piece of paper.

Paul Pereda

is an illustrator who has primarily worked in video game development and trading card games with clients such as Disney, Nickelodeon, Atari, and MTV. Born in Venezuela, he now lives in Madrid. He has been passionate about drawing since he was a child; his mother carried drawing supplies everywhere they went to keep him busy and calm.

Publisher & Creative Director
Ilona Oppenheim

Art Director & Designer
Jefferson Quintana
ILONA Creative Studio

Editor
Andrea Gollin

Writing Credits
Interview with Kitty O'Meara: **Andrea Gollin**

Printing
**Printed and bound in China by
Shenzhen Reliance Printers**

Cover
Illustration: **Stefano Di Cristofaro** and **Paul Pereda**
Cover design: **Jefferson Quintana**

Website
Visit www.andthepeoplestayedhomebook.com for further information,
activities, a teacher's guide, and more

Copyright ©2020 Tra Publishing
Poem text copyright © 2020 Kitty O'Meara
And the People Stayed Home first published in the United States by Tra Publishing
All rights reserved. No part of this publication may be reproduced or transmitted in any form
or by any means, electronic or mechanical, including photocopy, recording, or any other
information storage-and-retrieval system, without written permission from Tra Publishing.

ISBN: 978-1-7347617-8-8
Third Printing, November 2020
"And the People Stayed Home" by Kitty O'Meara. First published as "In the Time
of Pandemic" in the-daily-round.com. Also published in *Together in a Sudden Strangeness:
America's Poets Respond to the Pandemic* (Alfred A. Knopf). Tra Publishing is concurrently
releasing an ebook of *And the People Stayed Home* and is partnering with Vooks to
create a read-along, animated version. Words copyright © Kitty O'Meara.

And the People Stayed Home is printed on Forest Stewardship Council
certified paper from well-managed forests.

Tra Publishing is committed to sustainability in its materials and practices.

Tra Publishing
245 NE 37th Street
Miami, FL 33137
trapublishing.com

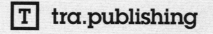

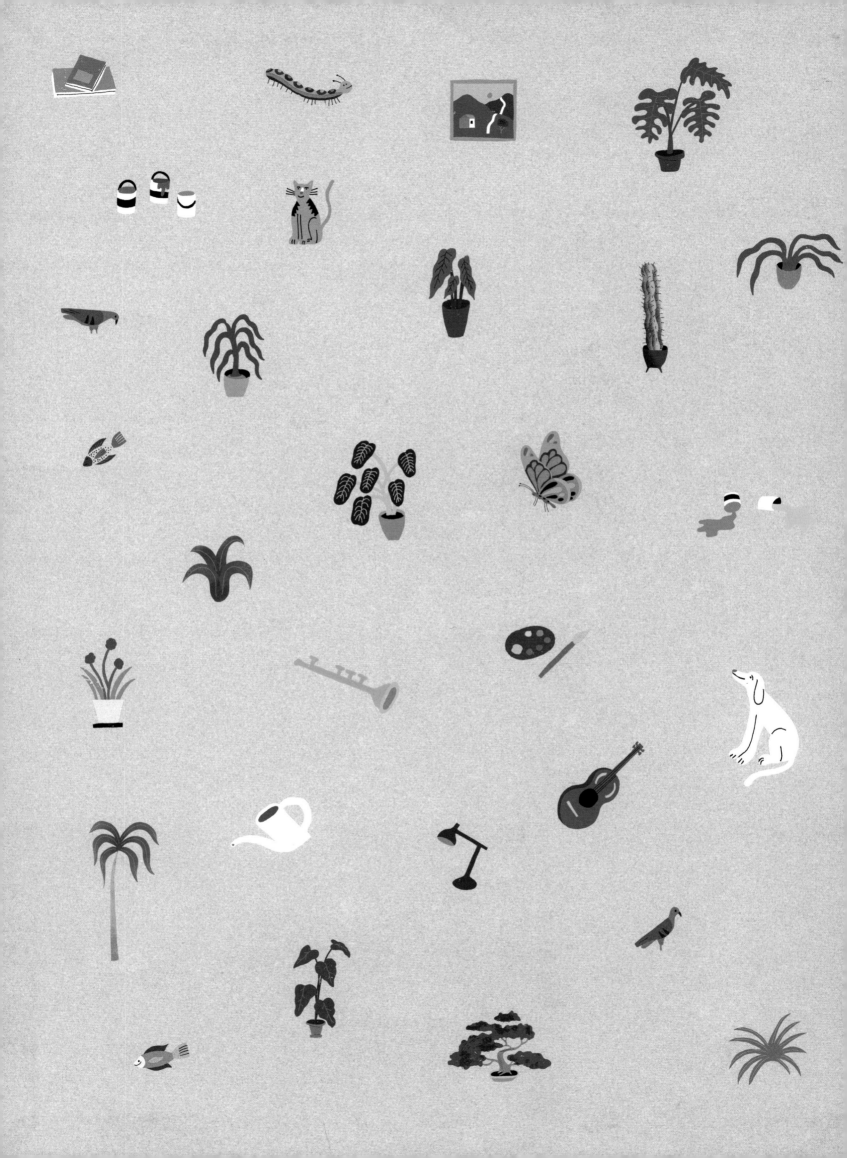